Last Lemonade Standing

Don't miss a single

Nancy Drew
Clue Book

#1: *Pool Party Puzzler*

Nancy Drew
* CLUE BOOK *

#2

Last Lemonade Standing

BY CAROLYN KEENE * ILLUSTRATED BY PETER FRANCIS

Aladdin
NEW YORK   LONDON   TORONTO   SYDNEY   NEW DELHI

ALADDIN

An imprint of Simon & Schuster Children's Publishing Division
1230 Avenue of the Americas, New York, NY 10020
This Aladdin paperback edition July 2015
Text copyright © 2015 by Simon & Schuster, Inc.
Illustrations copyright © 2015 by Peter Francis
Also available in an Aladdin hardcover edition.
All rights reserved, including the right of reproduction in whole or in part in any form.
ALADDIN is a trademark of Simon & Schuster, Inc., and related logo is a
registered trademark of Simon & Schuster, Inc.
NANCY DREW, NANCY DREW CLUE BOOK, and colophons are registered trademarks of
Simon & Schuster, Inc.
For information about special discounts for bulk purchases, please contact Simon & Schuster Special Sales
at 1-866-506-1949 or business@simonandschuster.com.
The Simon & Schuster Speakers Bureau can bring authors to your live event. For more
information or to book an event contact the Simon & Schuster Speakers Bureau
at 1-866-248-3049 or visit our website at www.simonspeakers.com.
Book designed by Karina Granda
The text of this book was set in Adobe Garamond Pro.
Manufactured in the United States of America 0117 OFF
4 6 8 10 9 7 5
Library of Congress Control Number 2015937522
ISBN 978-1-4814-3897-1 (hc)
ISBN 978-1-4814-3748-6 (pbk)
ISBN 978-1-4814-3749-3 (eBook)

* CONTENTS *

Chapter

SOUR POWER

"I don't get it," eight-year-old Nancy Drew said. "Doesn't anyone want lemonade?"

Nancy sat with her two best friends behind their lemonade stand. The table holding a pitcher of lemonade and paper cups was set up in the Drews' front yard.

"Maybe it's too hot," Bess Marvin suggested.

"We're selling ice-cold lemonade, Bess," George Fayne groaned. "Not hot cocoa!"

Nancy counted the few quarters and dimes

in a glass jar. She then wrote the total on her favorite writing pad with the ladybug design.

"At the rate we're going," Nancy said with a sigh, "we'll never earn enough money to buy Katy Sloan tickets."

Bess and George sighed too. Katy Sloan was their favorite singer. When they had heard that Katy's next concert would be at the River Heights Amusement Park, they knew they had to go. But Nancy, Bess, and George had already gone to the amusement park twice that summer to ride the rides. Both times their parents had paid for the tickets. So they would have to buy these tickets with their own money.

That's when Nancy had the idea for a lemonade stand. They even taped a picture of Katy to the table to make them work harder! Bess had written the date of the concert right on it.

"We've been selling lemonade for two whole days," Nancy said.

"And I know our lemonade is good enough," Bess insisted. "I got the recipe from my Pixie Scout cookbook!"

"Maybe that's the problem, Bess," George said. "Sometimes good enough isn't enough."

Nancy glanced over her shoulder at her house.

"If only Hannah would give us her top-secret recipe for pink-strawberry lemonade," Nancy said. "It's awesome!"

"Top secret?" Bess said, her blue eyes wide.

"Even from you?" George asked Nancy. "Hannah has been your housekeeper since you were four years old."

"*Three* years old!" Nancy corrected. "And Hannah is more than a housekeeper—she's like a mother to me."

"Then why won't she give you her recipe?" Bess asked.

"I told you, it's top secret!" Nancy said. She flashed a little smile. "Even from detectives like us!"

When Nancy, Bess, and George weren't selling lemonade they were part of a detective club called the Clue Crew. Nancy even had a special Clue Book so she could write down clues and suspects.

"Speaking of detective stuff," George said with a smile. "I joined the Spy Girl Gadget of the Month Club."

"You joined a club without us?" Bess gasped. "But Nancy is your best friend—and I'm your best cousin!"

"Are you *sure* you two are cousins?" Nancy joked.

Bess and George *were* cousins, but totally different.

Bess had blond hair, blue eyes, and a closet full of fashion-forward clothes. George had dark hair and eyes and liked her nickname better than her real name, Georgia. George's closet was full too—with electronic gadgets!

"The Spy Girl Gadget of the Month Club isn't really a club, Bess," George explained. "I just get a new spy gadget in the mail once a month."

George held up a purple pen and said, "The first gadget came yesterday. It's called a Presto Pen."

"What does it do?" Nancy asked.

"I don't know," George admitted. "I think my little brother, Scott, took the instructions—just like he takes everything else that belongs to me—"

"You guys, look!" Bess interrupted.

Nancy turned to see where Bess was pointing. Walking toward their lemonade stand were Andrea Wu, Bobby Wozniak, and Ben Washington from their third-grade class at school.

"Customers!" Nancy said. She smoothed her reddish-blond hair with her hands and whispered, "Everybody, smile!"

The kids approached, each wearing a READY, SET, COOK! T-shirt.

"'Ready, set, cook,'" Nancy read out loud. "Isn't that the kids' cooking show on TV?"

"Exactly!" Andrea said proudly. "You're looking at one of the next teams on the show—Team Lollipop!"

"Neat!" Bess said. "What are you going to cook?"

"Our challenge is to put together a picnic basket," Ben explained. "We're making chicken salad on rolls, potato salad, crunchy coleslaw, and pecan bars."

Nancy was surprised to see Bobby on the team. Bobby's nickname was Buggy because he loved bugs!

"You like to cook, Buggy?" Nancy asked.

"Not really," Bobby said. "My mom made me join the cooking show so I'd stop thinking about bugs this summer."

"How about some lemonade?" Bess asked.

"I'd rather have bug juice!" Buggy sighed.

"I'll have a cup, please," Ben said with a smile.

"One cup coming up!" George said. She picked up the pitcher and carefully poured lemonade into a paper cup. Ben drank it in one gulp.

"Not bad," Ben said, smacking his lips. "I taste lemons, sugar, water, and a small dash of vanilla extract."

"You tasted all that?" Nancy exclaimed.

"I can taste anything and name each ingredient!" Ben said proudly. "Superheroes have X-ray vision, but I have X-ray taste buds."

"Wow!" George said. She offered Andrea a cup, but she shook her head.

"No, thanks," Andrea said. "I just had a cup at Lily Ramos's lemonade stand."

Nancy, Bess, and George knew Lily from school. They also knew that Lily's Aunt Maria owned a chain of famous coffee-and-tea cafés called Beans and Bags.

"What's Lily's lemonade like?" Nancy asked.

"Pretty sour," Andrea said, scrunching her nose. "But her lemonade stand rocks!"

The girls traded surprised looks as Team Lollipop walked away.

"What could be so special about Lily's lemonade stand?" Bess wondered.

"There's only one way to find out," Nancy said. "Let's go over to Lily's house and check it out."

Nancy wrote BE RIGHT BACK on her ladybug pad. After putting the lemonade pitcher in the kitchen fridge, the girls made their way to Lily Ramos's house two blocks away.

Nancy, Bess, and George each had the same rule: They could walk anywhere as long as it wasn't more than five blocks away and as long as they were together. They didn't mind. Being together was more fun anyway!

"Whoa!" George gasped when they reached the Ramoses' front yard.

Behind Lily's lemonade stand were cushy chairs and a rolling book cart for customers.

There were board games on tiny tables and a FREE WI-FI sign.

When Lily saw Nancy, Bess, and George, she smiled.

"*This* is your lemonade stand, Lily?" Nancy asked.

"I like to call it a lemonade *experience*!"

Lily said. "My aunt Maria told me exactly what to do."

As Lily gave the girls a tour of her yard, she said, "It's also pet friendly . . . and for your sipping pleasure, my cousin Carlos will play his recorder!"

Nancy watched as Lily's six-year-old cousin strolled by, playing "Twinkle, Twinkle, Little Star." She then noticed something else. The prices of the lemonade, cupcakes, and cookies were written on the same ladybug paper she owned.

"Andrea was right," Nancy whispered to Bess and George. "Lily's lemonade stand really does rock."

But when they tried Lily's lemonade, their faces puckered up. Andrea was right about something else—Lily's lemonade was too sour!

"Don't you like it?" Lily asked.

"Um . . . it just needs a little something," Nancy said nicely.

"Like magic!" George joked.

"It's just that we have a lemonade stand too, Lily!" Bess said quickly.

"And your lemonade is better than mine?" Lily cried.

"Not better," Nancy said slowly. "Just . . . different."

Lily was still frowning as she left to help a customer. But as the girls walked out of Lily's yard, they were frowning too.

"No wonder we have no customers," Nancy said. "All the kids in River Heights are going to Lily's lemonade stand."

"You mean lemonade *experience*," George said. "Nobody seems to care that the lemonade tastes like swamp water."

"How are we going to sell enough lemonade for Katy Sloan tickets," Bess asked, "when everyone is buying from Lily?"

Nancy gave it some thought. There was only one way to bring customers to their lemonade stand.

"We need the most awesome lemonade

in the whole world, that's how!" Nancy announced.

"Where are we going to find that?" Bess wondered.

"By asking Hannah," Nancy said with a smile, "for her top-secret recipe for pink-strawberry lemonade!"

Chapter

TOP SECRET!

"Please, Hannah?" Nancy said. "Pretty please with sugar on top . . . and a strawberry?"

"Why don't I make the lemonade for you?" Hannah suggested. "Without telling you the recipe?"

"Thanks, Hannah," Nancy said. "But we really want to make our own lemonade for our own lemonade stand!"

The girls held their breaths while Hannah thought. Would she finally reveal the secret

Gruen family recipe for pink-strawberry lemonade?

"Everyone in my family had to promise to keep our recipe secret," Hannah said. "So you have to promise too!"

"Does that mean yes?" Nancy gasped.

"Only if you promise," Hannah said.

"We promise!" Nancy, Bess, and George said together.

"Okay then," Hannah said. "Grab a pen and paper and write down the ingredients."

Nancy remembered her ladybug notepad in her pocket. But when she looked around for a pen, she couldn't find one.

"Use this," George said. She handed Nancy her Presto Pen.

"Thanks, George," Nancy said. She then stood behind the kitchen counter ready to write the secret ingredients.

Hannah paced back and forth calling out the ingredients: lemons, strawberries, crushed mint leaves, both flat water and fizzy water to give it a little zip. . . .

"And last but not least," Hannah said, "two tablespoons of honey instead of sugar. That's what makes it special."

Nancy carefully wrote the ingredients and measurements. When she was done, she looked up and said, "Thanks a million, Hannah!"

After giving Hannah a big hug, Nancy ran to the calendar on the kitchen wall. She drew a heart around the date of Katy Sloan's concert— four days away. Would it be enough time to earn ticket money?

"Katy Sloan concert, here we come!" Nancy declared. She was about to return the Presto Pen when George shook her head.

"Keep the Presto Pen for

now, Nancy," George said. "Maybe it'll bring us good luck."

The girls walked together to the supermarket for lemonade ingredients. Once there they used two shopping carts. Since the recipe was top secret, they didn't want anyone to see all of the ingredients in one cart. They even spoke in secret code.

"Do we have enough aw-berries-stray?" Nancy whispered.

"Four baskets of aw-berries-stray," Bess said.

"On to the oney-hey," George whispered.

"The what?" Bess asked.

"The honey, Bess!" George said.

"Shhh!" Nancy hissed. "It's top secret!"

Nancy and George pushed both carts up the aisle. Bess pointed to a shelf with lemon-shaped jars. They were filled with Lickety-Split instant-lemonade powder.

"Look," Bess said. "Lickety-Split makes pink-strawberry lemonade, too!"

"It can't be as good as ours," Nancy said as

she held up Hannah's recipe. "That's a mix and ours is fresh."

Then as the girls walked under a whirling ceiling fan—*whoosh*—the wind blew the recipe out of Nancy's hand!

"Hannah's recipe!" Nancy cried as the paper shot up the aisle. "We have to get it before someone sees it!"

"But we can't leave our carts!" George said. "Or someone will see the ingredients!"

Pushing their carts, the girls chased the flyaway recipe until a boy stepped out from behind a tower of cereal boxes. It was Henderson "Drippy" Murphy from school.

Henderson's dad was Mr. Drippy the ice-cream man. Mr. Drippy's truck was a huge part of summer in River Heights.

"What's this?" Henderson asked, picking up the recipe.

George snatched the recipe from his hand and said, "It's our shopping list. No biggie."

"Whatever," Henderson said with a shrug.

He was wearing a T-shirt with Katy Sloan's picture on the front!

"Do you like Katy Sloan too?" Nancy asked.

"I don't like *her*," Henderson said, his cheeks blushing. "I just like her music, that's all."

Henderson then pointed to the lemons in one of the shopping carts. "But I *hate* lemons!" he said angrily.

"Why?" Bess asked.

"My dad traded his ice-cream truck for a dumb lemonade shake-up truck," Henderson explained. "What's so special about lemonade anyway?"

"*Our* lemonade will be special!" Bess blurted excitedly. "We're making pink—"

George clapped her hand over Bess's mouth before she could say more. Henderson shrugged again, then walked away.

"You almost spilled our secret, Bess!" George said.

"But she didn't!" Nancy said with a smile. "Now let's find the rest of the ingredients and get to work."

Nancy, Bess, and George spent the rest of the day squeezing lemons, blending strawberries, and measuring honey. By dinnertime they had three pitchers of Hannah's pink-strawberry lemonade. The girls each took a test-sip. . . .

"Yum!" George said.

"Yummy!" Nancy added.

"Yummy for the tummy!" Bess exclaimed.

The girls traded high fives. Their lemonade

was awesome. Hopefully their customers tomorrow would think so too!

"You guys," Nancy said excitedly the next morning. "We're lemonade superstars!"

Nancy still couldn't believe it as she poured another cup of cold pink-strawberry lemonade. They had set up their stand just an hour ago, and they already had served ten customers!

"Giving out samples of our lemonade was a great idea, George," Nancy said as more kids lined up. "Everybody is coming back for more."

"With their friends!" Bess pointed out.

Nancy had remembered to tape their picture of Katy Sloan on the table next to the iced sugar cookies that Hannah had baked for them to sell. She was about to brush away some crumbs when one more customer stepped up to the table. . . .

"Lily!" Nancy said with surprise. "Why aren't you at your own lemonade stand—I mean, lemonade experience?"

"I heard your lemonade is awesome," Lily said. She bought a cup, took a sip, and gasped. "This *is* awesome. How did you make it?"

"Sorry," George said. "Our lips are zipped."

Lily frowned before walking away. Nancy had no time to wonder if Lily was jealous. They had thirsty kids to feed!

"What if we run out of lemonade?" Bess asked.

"I still have the recipe if we need to make more," Nancy said, holding up her ladybug paper. "Can you put it in your messenger bag so it's safe, Bess?"

Bess took the recipe just as a bunch of kids walked over. This time it was Henderson followed by Team Lollipop.

"I'll get more cups!" George said happily. As she ran back to the house, Henderson stepped up to the stand.

"I heard your lemonade rocks," Henderson said. He nodded at the pitcher. "But why is it pink?"

"It's pink-strawberry lemonade!" Nancy said proudly.

"Strawberry?" Henderson cried his eyes wide. "Nobody told me it was *strawberry* lemonade!"

Nancy and Bess were surprised too. What was Henderson's problem? But then—

"We're in a hurry," Andrea said as she stepped in front of Henderson. "We have to be at the TV studio soon. *Ready, Set, Cook!* starts filming at three o'clock!"

"And we're going to win the summer picnic-basket contest!" Ben added excitedly.

George hurried back, her arms overflowing with more paper cups. Bess took three and began to pour.

"Three cups, coming up!" Bess declared.

Andrea and Buggy sipped their lemonade first. They thought it was the best ever. Bess was about to pour Ben's cup when George shook her head.

"Don't, Bess!" George whispered. "If Ben tastes our lemonade, he'll know the secret ingredients!"

"Ben has X-ray taste buds!" Nancy added.

"Um . . . what's up?" Ben asked.

The girls traded looks. They had to keep Ben from tasting their secret strawberry lemonade—but how?

"Uh . . . I . . . just saw a bug inside the pitcher," Nancy said, thinking fast. "No more lemonade until we get it out."

"A bug?" Buggy said excitedly. "What kind? Where?"

In a flash Buggy reached out, knocking the pitcher and plate of cookies off the table.

"Now I'll never get to see the bugs!" Buggy pouted.

Bess and George groaned as the last of the lemonade trickled onto the grass. But Nancy was more worried about the cookies. Some of them had chocolate icing on top. What if her puppy, Chocolate Chip, ate them? Chocolate was dangerous for dogs to eat.

"Pick up the cookies!" Nancy said. "Before Chip finds them!"

Nancy, Bess, and George bent down to pick up the cookies. By the time they stood up, Team Lollipop was gone. Walking away from the stand was Henderson, stuffing something into his pocket.

"We can make more lemonade, Henderson!" Nancy called.

"No, thanks!" Henderson called back.

Nancy watched as Henderson hurried out

of the yard and up the block. What was his rush? Suddenly—

"Omigosh!" Bess cried. "I put Hannah's recipe here on the table before I poured the lemonade. And now . . . and now . . ."

Nancy stared at Bess. Her heart began to pound as she thought the worst.

"Hannah's recipe is gone?" Nancy cried.

"Well, yes . . . and no," Bess said. She held up the ladybug paper. "The paper is still here . . . but the *recipe* is gone!"

Chapter

RECIPE FOR TROUBLE

Nancy, Bess, and George stared at the ladybug paper. It was totally blank!

"What happened to Hannah's recipe?" Nancy exclaimed.

"Maybe someone switched the recipe with the same ladybug paper," George suggested. "A blank piece of ladybug paper!"

"That means Hannah's secret recipe for pink-strawberry lemonade was *stolen*!" Nancy gasped.

"And it's my fault!" Bess cried. "I was going to put the recipe in my bag, but when things got busy I forgot!"

Nancy shook her head and said, "It's my fault. I should never have taken Hannah's recipe out of my pocket!"

"Who cares whose fault it is?" George said. "Nancy, how are you going to tell Hannah her top-secret lemonade recipe was stolen?"

Nancy's stomach did a double flip. Could she really tell Hannah that her recipe was stolen after they had promised to keep it a secret?

"We can't tell Hannah!" Nancy blurted. "Not until I find the person who took the recipe."

"Why, Nancy?" Bess asked slowly. "Whoever took the recipe already knows the secret ingredients."

"I know," Nancy said sadly. "But maybe the recipe thief will promise to keep it a secret too."

"It's worth a try," George said.

Nancy nodded and said, "The Clue Book

is in my room. Let's clean up here, then get to work."

"The Clue Book?" George said with a grin. "I know what that means."

"So do I," Bess said. "It means the Clue Crew is on the case!"

Nancy, Bess, and George carried their lemonade stand supplies into the kitchen.

"Closing your stand so soon?" Hannah asked, surprised. "Didn't the kids like my top-secret lemonade recipe?"

The girls traded looks. What would they tell Hannah?

"Um—the kids loved it, Hannah!" Nancy said. "But then . . . then . . ."

"It got too hot for lemonade!" George piped in.

"How could it be too hot for ice-cold lemonade?" Hannah asked.

"If all our ice melted?" Bess blurted.

The girls left the kitchen and hurried up the stairs. Nancy felt awful for not telling Hannah the truth. But she couldn't—not yet!

Once they were in Nancy's room, the girls huddled around the Clue Book. Nancy opened it to a clean page. Then, using the pen George lent her, she wrote the name of their new case:

Who Took Hannah's Top-Secret Recipe for Pink-Strawberry Lemonade?

Underneath that, she wrote:

Suspects.

"It's got to be Henderson 'Drippy' Murphy," George said. "I saw him stuff something inside his pocket when he left our lemonade stand."

"I saw it too," Nancy said.

"I saw it three!" Bess added.

"Did you also see how weird Henderson acted when he found out that our lemonade was strawberry-flavored?" Nancy asked.

"Maybe Henderson wanted a pink-strawberry recipe for his dad's lemonade truck," Bess suggested. "But what would he be doing with ladybug paper?"

Nancy thought hard. Maybe the recipe thief didn't switch the ladybug papers.

"Maybe I accidentally wrote the recipe on two pieces of ladybug paper stuck together," Nancy explained. "Henderson could have taken the top sheet, leaving a blank one underneath."

Nancy wrote Henderson's name in the Clue Book. His was the first name on her suspect list.

Henderson

"The Clue Crew has a suspect!" George said with a grin. "Sweet!"

Bess's eyes popped wide open. "George, did you say 'sweet'?" she asked.

"Yeah, so?" George said.

"Sweet makes me think of Team Lollipop!" Bess said excitedly. "They were at our stand right before the recipe went missing."

"Team Lollipop could have taken the recipe while we were picking up the cookies," George said with a nod.

"Buggy probably has ladybug paper too!" Bess added. She wrinkled her nose. "Anything to do with bugs!"

But Nancy wasn't too sure about Team Lollipop.

"Why would Team Lollipop want our lemonade recipe?" Nancy asked. "It's not like they have a lemonade stand."

"Lily Ramos has a lemonade stand," George said. "And she has the exact same ladybug paper, too."

"But Lily left right after she tasted our lemonade," Bess said.

"Lily could have hid somewhere," George said. "To secretly snoop on us and our lemonade stand."

"Lily said our lemonade was awesome," Nancy added. "Maybe she wanted the recipe for her own lemonade stand!"

"You mean lemonade *experience*!" Bess giggled.
Nancy added Lily's name to their suspect list.

Lily

She then shut the Clue Book and said, "Let's go outside and see if we can find some clues."

The three girls slipped past Hannah and out the front door. The table they had used for their lemonade stand was still in the front yard.

"Our picture of Katy Sloan is gone," Bess noticed, pointing to the table.

"The wind probably blew it away," George said. "I should have used more tape."

Nancy spotted a piece of paper on the grass. It wasn't their picture of Katy—it looked like some kind of list.

Nancy picked up the paper and studied it.

"Bess, George," Nancy said. "This is a list of the food that's going into Team Lollipop's picnic basket!"

"You mean for the TV show *Ready, Set, Cook!*?" Bess asked.

"It must be what Andrea put on the table when she paid for her lemonade," George said. "So what's cookin'?"

"Yummy stuff!" Nancy said as she smiled down at the list. "There's chicken salad on rolls, crunchy coleslaw, potato salad, lemonade—"

Nancy stopped midsentence. Did she just see what she thought she saw?

Was Team Lollipop making *lemonade*?

Chapter

COOKS . . . OR CROOKS?

The Clue Crew huddled around Team Lollipop's list. At the end *was* the word "lemonade"!

"They didn't say they were making lemonade yesterday," Nancy said.

"They're making it now!" George said. "What better way to win a cooking contest than with the best pink-strawberry lemonade recipe in the world?"

"How do we know it's Hannah's recipe?" ～～ asked.

Nancy knew how they could find out. She looked at her watch. It was one thirty.

"Andrea said that the contest starts filming at three o'clock," Nancy said. "We should go to the TV station too."

"But we're not on a team!" Bess said. "They'll never let us in!"

"My mom is a caterer and works with lots of chefs," George said, her eyes lighting up. "Chefs mean chefs' *hats*!"

"Chefs' hats, huh?" Nancy repeated slowly. "I like it. I like it."

The Clue Crew was about to go undercover!

"How do people cook with these things on?" Bess complained an hour later. "This hat keeps flopping in my face!"

"They're chefs' hats for grown-ups, Bess," George said. "So *grow up* and quit complaining!"

Nancy carried a wicker picnic basket as the Clue Crew approached Station WRIV-TV. After filing through the front door, the girls were greeted by a guard. Her last name was embroidered on her jacket: BROWN.

"Can I help you?" Ms. Brown asked from behind her desk.

"We're here for the *Ready, Set, Cook!* show," Nancy said, flashing a big smile.

"That's why we're dressed like chefs!" Bess explained.

Ms. Brown raised an eyebrow and said, "And what's the name of your team?"

"Um—Team Broccoli!" George blurted.

"Ew—not broccoli, George!" Bess cried. She smiled at Ms. Brown and said, "It's Team Cupcake!"

"I happen to like broccoli, Bess!" George hissed. But Ms. Brown wasn't buying it one bit.

"If you're Team Cupcake," Ms. Brown said. "Why do your hats read 'Louise Fayne Catering'?"

Gulp! Nancy, Bess, and George rolled their eyes up to their hats. They hadn't thought of that!

"Because . . . it's good advertising for my mom?" George said. "She's a caterer."

Bess stepped forward. She pointed to the picnic basket in Nancy's hand.

"Excuse me, Ms. Brown," Bess said. "We have ice cream in here. If we don't get to the studio soon, you'll have a mint chocolate-chip puddle on your floor!"

Nancy tried not to giggle. Their basket was really empty—but Bess's idea seemed to be working!

"Okay, okay," Ms. Brown said pointing down a long hallway. "*Ready, Set, Cook!* is shot in Studio B."

"Thank you!" Bess said sweetly.

Nancy, Bess, and George raced down the hall to the door marked Studio B. But when they stepped inside the studio, it was dark and empty.

"Where is everybody?" Nancy asked.

There were TV cameras, lights hanging from the ceiling, and three big, shiny cooking counters. But no people!

"It's better empty," George said. "Now we can look for clues without anyone knowing."

The Clue Crew headed straight for the cooking counters. Each one had a sign reading one of the names of the three teams.

"'Team Popsicle,' 'Team Pepperoni,'" Bess read out loud. "And 'Team Lollipop'!"

Nancy, Bess, and George ran to Team Lollipop's cooking counter. It was big enough to hold the cooking ingredients for the contest plus mixing bowls and spoons of all sizes.

"Here's a bowl of lemons," Nancy said, picking up the bowl. "Now we *know* they're making lemonade!"

"Check it out!" George said. She reached under the counter to pull a square plastic container off a shelf. Written on the lid were the words "Top Secret!"

"Top secret?" Nancy said. She put down the bowl to look at the container. "Why would it say that?"

"Maybe it's Hannah's recipe!" Bess said excitedly. "It's so good they don't want anyone else to know what's in it!"

"I'm opening it!" George said. But just as she was about to pop the lid—

FLASH!

Nancy, Bess, and George jumped as the huge lights suddenly came on all at once.

"I hear voices outside the door!" George whispered. "Somebody is coming!"

The girls didn't want anyone to know they

were snooping. So they ducked under the counter seconds before the studio door swung open. The counter was big enough to hide all three girls and their basket underneath.

Carefully, the girls peeked out. They could see people filing through the door into the studio. They were grown-ups wearing headsets, a man dressed in a jacket and tie, and the three cooking teams.

"The guy in a jacket is the host of the show," Nancy whispered. "His name is Gordon Whimsy."

"I know," Bess whispered. "He's strict with the teams!"

"But he's an awesome cook," George whispered, the top-secret container clutched in her hand.

One woman began calling out orders to the crew. Nancy guessed she was the director of *Ready, Set, Cook!*

"Okay, people!" the woman shouted. "That last-minute tech meeting put us all behind schedule, so everybody get in their places so we can start shooting the contest!"

"Sure, Ellen!" the stage manager said with a smile.

But Gordon wasn't smiling as he groaned, "Delays, delays. Nothing but delays!"

The girls froze as three pairs of legs appeared outside the counter. It was Team Lollipop, ready to cook!

"Hey!" Andrea said. "That's not where I put the lemon bowl."

"And where's my secret box?" Buggy said.

"What secret box?" Ben asked.

"Um . . . nothing," Buggy replied.

Nancy, Bess, and George traded puzzled looks under the counter. Did only Buggy know about the box?

"Quiet, everyone, please!" the stage manager shouted before counting down. "Three . . . two . . . one!"

The show's opening tune blasted through the studio. After that the voice of an announcer boomed: "Hey, let's get cooking, kids, because it's time for—"

"READY! SET! COOK!" the three teams yelled out.

Nancy, Bess, and George peeked out to see Gordon smiling straight at the camera.

"I'm your host, Gordon Whimsy," Gordon said cheerily. "Now that you've met me, let's meet our cooking-good teams!"

From the corner of her eye Nancy saw George fumbling with the secret box.

"What are you doing?" Nancy whispered.

"Trying to open this secret box!" George whispered. "If the recipe is inside, I want to know!"

The box popped open. George stared

into it. She then sucked her breath in softly.

"Is it our recipe, George?" Bess whispered.

"Nope," George whispered back.

"What is it?" Nancy whispered.

"It's . . . ants!" George gulped.

Chapter

GETTING ANTSY

"Ants?" Nancy hissed. She, Bess, and George peered inside the container. It *was* filled with ants. About a dozen of them!

"Gross!" Bess hissed. "Close the lid—quick!"

Bess reached out to shut the container. Instead she knocked the container out of George's hand. It fell on the floor with a *plunk*, spilling the creepy-crawly ants onto the floor!

An army of ants crawled straight toward Team Lollipop's feet just as they were being interviewed by Gordon Whimsy!

"And here's a team that's hard to lick—Team Lollipop!" Gordon announced. "Kids, what will be in your picnic basket today?"

"Ants!" Andrea screamed.

"Pardon me?" Gordon asked.

"I've got ants crawling up my leg!" Andrea shouted.

"And I've got ants up my pants!" Ben cried.

The girls crawled out from under the table— before the rest of the ants could crawl all over them!

"Nancy? Bess? George?" Andrea cried, shaking her leg. "What are you doing here?"

Nancy was about to explain when Ellen the director charged out of the control room.

"I said, 'Cut!'" Ellen cried. "I want to know how those ants got into this studio!"

Nancy knew they had to tell the truth.

"They were in a box marked top secret," Nancy explained. "George opened it while we were hiding under the table."

"Why were you hiding under the table?" Ellen asked.

"We're detectives," Nancy explained. "Somebody stole our recipe for pink-strawberry lemonade and—"

"And you thought it was us?" Ben demanded as he slapped his pants legs silly.

"Not anymore!" Bess said. She pointed to the ingredients on Team Lollipop's table. "There are no strawberries on the table at all. And you're using sugar instead of—"

This time Bess clapped her own hand over

her mouth before she could say "honey."

Nancy studied the ingredients on Team Lollipop's table. Bess was right. No strawberries. No honey. Team Lollipop couldn't be making Hannah's recipe without those.

"Excuse me," Buggy said. "But can we start collecting my ants, please?"

Everyone turned to stare at Buggy.

"Your ants?" Gordon demanded. "Why on earth did you bring ants to a cooking show?"

"Because we're making a picnic basket," Buggy replied. "And what's a picnic without ants?"

"Give me a break!" Andrea groaned.

"Thanks a lot, Bug Boy!" Ben snapped at Buggy. "You just lost the contest for Team Lollipop."

"Well, that explains how the ants got in here," Ellen said. She looked straight at Nancy, Bess, and George. "Now why don't you girls tell me how *you* got in here?"

Before Nancy, Bess, or George could speak, Gordon pointed to the girls' hats.

"Does that say Louise Fayne Catering?" Gordon exclaimed. "I worked there right after cooking school."

"Louise is my mom," George said.

"And my aunt!" Bess added with a smile.

"Brilliant!" Gordon exclaimed. "I loved working for Louise Fayne!"

He turned to Ellen and said, "These girls meant no harm. It was that Buggy boy who brought those ants here."

"Sorry," Buggy said with a shrug. "I told my mom I'd rather be in the Bug Club."

A boy on Team Pepperoni raised his hand. "Are we ever going to start this contest?" he asked.

"Yeah," a girl on Team Popsicle said. "Our Quickie-Queso Cheese Dip is getting lumpy!"

Everyone listened as Ellen made an announcement. The contest would be taped the next morning when the studio was sure to be bug free.

"We're sorry that we caused trouble," Nancy

admitted. "We just have to find who stole our secret recipe."

She turned to Team Lollipop and said, "It's definitely not you guys."

Nancy dragged the picnic basket out from under the table. Before they could leave, Gordon invited all three girls to be on the show next summer. As Nancy, Bess, and George left the studio they could hardly believe it.

"Us on *Ready, Set, Cook!*?" Bess said excitedly. "I can't wait until next year!"

"What do you think we should make?" Nancy asked.

"Anything but lemonade!" George groaned.

Nancy, Bess, and George pulled off their hats and aprons and stuffed them into the picnic basket. It was the same place where Nancy had packed the Clue Book and pen.

"No ants inside the picnic basket." Nancy sighed with relief as she pulled out the Clue Book. "And Team Lollipop is innocent."

Nancy crossed Team Lollipop off the suspect list and said, "Now our suspects are Henderson 'Drippy' Murphy and Lily Ramos."

"Let's walk past Lily's lemonade stand on our way home," George said. "Maybe we'll find more clues."

"As long as we don't find any more ants!" Bess said with a shiver. "Ick!"

But when the girls got to Lily's yard, there were no kids or lemonade. Only a CLOSED sign on the table.

"I wonder where Lily is," Nancy said.

The sound of music suddenly filled the air. The girls glanced back to see Lily's cousin Carlos sitting on the front doorstep playing his recorder.

"Let's see what he knows," George whispered.

"Hi, Carlos," Nancy said as the girls walked over. "Where's Lily?"

Carlos stopped playing to look up. "Lily and her mom went to the supermarket," he said.

"To buy stuff for dinner?" Nancy asked.

"To buy stuff for her lemonade tomorrow," Carlos explained. "Her new and improved lemonade!"

"New and improved?" Nancy said. "How is it going to be new and improved?"

Carlos shrugged. He went back to playing his recorder until George yanked it out of his mouth.

"Hey—that's mine!" Carlos whined.

"You'll get it back," George said. "First tell us what makes Lily's lemonade so new and improved."

"How should I know?" Carlos said. "I'm just the entertainment around here."

"You've got to know something, Carlos!" Bess said. "Put on your thinking cap, please."

Carlos scrunched up his nose as he thought hard. His eyes suddenly lit up. "Lily said something about her new lemonade being her favorite color."

"Her favorite color?" Nancy said. "What is Lily's favorite color?"

"That's easy!" Carlos said with a smile. "It's pink!"

Chapter

SQUEEZE OR TEASE?

"Pink?" Nancy, Bess, and George exclaimed.

"Is that your favorite color too?" Carlos asked.

Nancy didn't answer Carlos's question because she had one of her own. "When are they getting back, Carlos?" she asked.

"They might stop for pizza on the way home," Carlos replied. "Lucky ducks."

Nancy, Bess, and George all frowned. If Lily and her mom were stopping for dinner, it would take them forever to get home.

"Okay, Carlos. Thanks." Nancy sighed.

"Can I have my recorder back now?" Carlos asked. He puffed his chest out proudly. "I can play 'The Wheels on the Bus'—backward!"

George tossed the recorder back to Carlos. As he played, the girls walked away from the house.

"Let's meet here tomorrow at ten o'clock," Nancy said. "So we can question Lily."

"What should we do until then?" Bess asked.

"Think *pink*!" Nancy said with a smile.

The girls walked home together. They waved good-bye as they each reached their houses one by one.

When Nancy got home, she found Hannah in the kitchen making dinner. She also found a pitcher of pink-strawberry lemonade on the counter!

"I made a batch for you," Hannah said with a smile. "Just in case you get tired of squeezing lemons!"

Nancy forced a smile. She had to tell Hannah they weren't selling lemonade tomorrow—at least not until they found out who stole the secret recipe.

"Um . . . we're not selling lemonade tomorrow, Hannah," Nancy said. She held up the Clue Book. "We're solving a new mystery. See?"

"A new mystery?" Hannah asked. "Is something missing?"

"Well . . . yes," Nancy said. "Something . . . top secret."

"Top secret?" Hannah chuckled. She nodded at her pitcher of lemonade. "I know all about top secret; that's for sure!"

"For sure!" Nancy squeaked.

Hannah turned back to the lettuce she was washing at the sink. Nancy placed the Clue Book on the kitchen table. She then turned sadly to the calendar on the wall.

How will we ever see Katy Sloan's concert now? Nancy thought. But as she gazed at the concert date, something wasn't right. The heart she had drawn on the calendar was *gone*!

Nancy's thoughts were interrupted by the voice of her dad calling, "I'm home!"

Mr. Drew walked into the kitchen. He smiled as he pulled off the tie he often wore for his job as a lawyer.

"Daddy, did you buy a new calendar?" Nancy asked as her dad kissed her on the cheek.

"A new calendar in the middle of the year?" Mr. Drew chuckled. "What made you think that?"

Nancy stared up at her dad. How could she tell him that the heart she had drawn on the calendar was gone? He would never believe her!

"Just wondering, Daddy," Nancy said quickly. She grabbed the Clue Book and pen, then hurried up to her room before dinner. Chip burst into her room too, hopping up onto Nancy's bed.

Sitting on the bed next to Chip, Nancy opened the Clue Book to a clean page. There she wrote:

Clue: Lily has a new recipe for pink lemonade. Investigate tomorrow!

Nancy shut the book. Did Lily Ramos really take Hannah's top-secret recipe for pink-strawberry lemonade?

"If it really is Lily, Chip," Nancy told her dog. "I hope she's good at keeping secrets." She petted Chip and sighed. "At least better than *me*!"

"Wow!" Nancy said the next morning as the Clue Crew approached the Ramoses' yard. There were more kids at Lily's lemonade experience than ever before.

Lily was also in her yard next to her lemonade table. "Get your fresh lemonade here . . . made from scratch!" she was shouting. "Get your fresh pink-strawberry lemonade!"

"Pink-strawberry, huh?" Nancy said. "So that's her new and improved lemonade."

Nancy, Bess, and George walked over to Lily.

"You didn't have pink-strawberry lemonade yesterday, Lily," George said. "Why the switch?"

"Your pink-strawberry lemonade gave me an idea," Lily replied with a shrug.

"An idea or a whole recipe?" Bess asked.

"What's in it, Lily?" Nancy asked.

"I can't tell you," Lily said. "If you'll excuse

me, I have more lemonade to pour. Business is through the roof!"

As Lily began pouring her pink-strawberry lemonade, Bess pointed to the table.

"Look at the jar holding the money," Bess whispered. "It's shaped like a lemon—just like the jar Lickety-Split Lemonade comes in."

Nancy stared at the jar. The label was washed off but the jar was exactly the same as Lickety-Split's!

"You guys," Nancy whispered. "Do you think Lily is serving instant lemonade and telling everyone she made it?"

"I know how we can find out," George said.

George waved Nancy and Bess toward the Ramoses' trash cans against the side of the house. She then pointed to the blue recycling can and said, "If Lily made all that lemonade, she would have used a lot of jars!"

George pulled up the lid. The girls then stood on their toes and peered inside. Sure enough, inside the can was a big pile of—

"Lickety-Split Lemonade jars!" Bess gasped.

"Lily's lemonade isn't Hannah's recipe," Nancy decided. "It's just Lickety-Split!"

George was about to shut the lid when—

"Hey! What are you doing back here?" someone demanded.

The girls whirled around to see Lily. She had both hands on her hips, and she didn't look happy!

Chapter

LICKETY-FIT

"Hi, Lily," Nancy blurted.

"Why were you snooping in our recycling can?" Lily demanded. "If you're looking for any of my old diaries you're out of luck!"

"We came to look for our pink-strawberry lemonade recipe," Nancy said. "It went missing yesterday."

"But you used Lickety-Split Lemonade," George said pointing to the recycling bins.

"Shh!" Lily cried. She lowered her voice.

"My customers think my lemonade is fresh—not a powder!"

"There's nothing wrong with Lickety-Split, Lily," Nancy said gently. "What's wrong is to tell everyone you made it from scratch when you didn't."

"I'm sure your aunt Maria wouldn't do that at her famous cafés," Bess added. "Would she?"

Lily began blinking hard. She then shook her head and said, "My aunt Maria does everything right. She's my hero!"

"So what are you going to do?" Nancy asked.

"I'm going to stop lying about my lemonade," Lily promised. "But I will keep selling Lickety-Split."

"Why?" George asked.

"Because I hate squeezing lemons, that's why!" Lily declared. "Did you ever squirt lemon juice in your eye by accident? Owie!"

Lily was about to return to her stand when Antonio Elefano from school walked over.

"Do you really allow pets here?" Antonio asked.

"Sure!" Lily said with a smile. "My lemonade experience is totally pet friendly."

"Cool!" Antonio said as he reached into his backpack. "Because I brought Stinky—my pet rat!"

Lily and Bess screamed as Antonio held up the squirming rat. When Stinky heard the screams, he jumped out of Antonio's hand onto the ground. When the other pets saw Stinky, they barked, meowed, and chased him through the yard!

"We'd better get out of here," Nancy told her friends. "Lickety-split!"

The girls left Lily's yard and headed toward Main Street. They had permission from their parents to buy frozen yogurt at their favorite store, Fro-Yo A-Go-Go.

"This place is the best," George said as she pulled the handle on the yogurt machine. "Where else can you fill your

own cup with any yogurt flavor you want?"

"And put on your own toppings!" Nancy added, squirting pistachio yogurt into her cup.

"Yogurt is yummy," Bess agreed. "But I'm sure going to miss Henderson's dad's ice-cream truck."

"Yeah." George sighed. "Mr. Drippy will probably be Mr. Squeezy now."

Nancy remembered Henderson stuffing something into his pocket as he left their lemonade stand.

"Henderson is the only suspect we have

left," Nancy said as they headed toward the topping counter. Suddenly a bunch of younger kids darted in front of them.

George recognized two of the boys, Mikey Pinsky and Victor Sung from her block.

"Mikey, Victor, hel-lo?" George called. "There's a line from the yogurt to the toppings!"

"We never got yogurt, smarty-pants," Mikey sneered. He pointed to the toppings. "Just this stuff."

"No yogurt?" Nancy asked with surprise.

Nancy, Bess, and George watched as the kids began loading their cups with gummy worms, licorice, tutti-frutti cereal, sprinkles, chocolate chips, raspberries, blueberries, pineapple chunks—the works!

"Hurry up, you guys," Victor told the others. "Henderson wants us back at his house in fifteen minutes!"

"Did you say Henderson?" Nancy asked the kids. "Are you talking about Henderson 'Drippy'—I mean—Murphy?"

The kids traded looks before Victor said, "We can't tell you. It's a secret."

"Does that secret have something to do with lemonade?" George demanded.

"How did you know?" a girl gasped.

Nancy, Bess, and George watched open-mouthed as the kids paid for their toppings and left.

"It *does* have something to do with lemonade," Nancy whispered. "We should follow them!"

"I know where Henderson lives," George agreed. "It's the house with the ice-cream cone–shaped mailbox!"

But Bess shook her head. "We're not going until I get my toppings," she insisted. "I can't eat fro-yo without blueberries and crispy coconut!"

"Okay," George said. "But after our fro-yo, we go-go straight to Henderson's!"

The girls poured on their toppings and ate their frozen yogurt. They then left the shop and quickly walked to Henderson's house.

Nancy, Bess, and George went to the front door. After they rang the doorbell several times, no one answered.

"Where is everybody?" Bess asked.

"Maybe the kids didn't go to Henderson's house," George said. "Maybe they just said that to trick us."

As they turned away from the door, Nancy noticed something way up in a nearby tree. . . .

"It's a tree house!" Nancy said, pointing. "Maybe Henderson and the kids are up there!"

They were about to head for the tree house when something round and yellow rolled out from under the garage door. It was a lemon!

Nancy looked at the lemon, then at the garage.

"Where there are lemons—there's lemonade," Nancy said, turning toward the garage. "Come on, Clue Crew. We're going in!"

Chapter

LEMON-RAID

The Clue Crew could hear voices inside the garage. When George rapped on the garage door, the chatter stopped.

"Is anybody in there?" George called.

"It depends," Henderson called back. "Who's there?"

"It's Nancy, Bess, and George," Nancy called. "We want to ask you something, Henderson."

"Not now," Henderson shouted. "We're busy in here."

"Too bad," George said through the door. "Because we have an awesome pizza with extra cheese that we want to share."

"Pizza?" excited voices cried. "Cool! Open the door, Henderson!"

The garage door slowly rose. Nancy, Bess, and George looked inside. There was no car, just Henderson and the kids from the yogurt shop. The kids were now wearing lab coats and goggles. They were standing behind a table filled with chemistry beakers!

"Wow!" Nancy exclaimed.

Also on the table were bowls filled with lemons and the toppings from the yogurt shop.

"Where's the pizza?" Victor asked.

"What pizza?" George said. She turned to Henderson and asked, "What's going on in here?"

Henderson shrugged as he mumbled, "Um . . . we're just whipping up a science experiment."

"It looks like you're whipping up lemonade!" Bess said.

"Okay!" Henderson sighed. "So you found my lemon lab."

"Lemon lab?" Nancy asked.

"We're trying to come up with thirty lemonade flavors," Henderson explained. "So my dad's lemonade truck will be just like an ice-cream truck!"

Henderson pointed to another table near the garage wall. On it were pitchers of lemonade in different colors.

"So far we made licorice lemonade, coconut lemonade, and pistachio lemonade!" Henderson said proudly.

"Don't forget spinach lemonade!" a girl with goggles added. "It's an acquired taste."

"I think I get it," Nancy said. "But why is your lemon lab such a big secret?"

"I want to surprise my dad!" Henderson replied.

The Clue Crew stepped back to whisper among themselves.

"One of those thirty flavors could be pink strawberry," Nancy said. "Let's look for our secret ingredients—and the missing recipe."

"Good idea," Bess whispered.

The Clue Crew strolled around the table studying fruit, candy, and vegetables. There was no honey, fizzy water, mint, strawberries, or recipe written on ladybug paper!

"Now what are you looking for?" Henderson asked.

"You were stuffing something in your pocket

when you left our lemonade stand," George explained. "What was it?"

"Something in my pocket?" Henderson gulped. "I don't know what you're talking about."

Henderson pointed to the open door and exclaimed, "Quit being nosy and get out of my lemon lab, Clue Crew!"

Mikey stood up with a lemon in each hand. "Or prepare for a squeeze attack!" he said with a grin.

The other kids stood up holding lemons too.

"Nancy, George, I can't get lemon juice on my new summer blouse!" Bess whispered. "Let's go . . . pleeeeeeease?"

Nancy, Bess, and George left the garage.

"They can't be making Hannah's secret recipe," Bess said as they walked away. "Not without strawberries, fizzy water, mint, or honey."

"But what was Henderson stuffing in his

pocket yesterday?" Nancy wondered. "I still want to know!"

As they approached Henderson's tree house, Nancy stopped. She looked up at the small house and smiled.

"Kids keep secret stuff in their tree houses all the time," Nancy said excitedly. "Maybe that's where Henderson put Hannah's secret recipe!"

The girls climbed the wooden ladder leading up to Henderson's tree house. One by one they stepped inside. . . .

"Holy cannoli!" George cried.

Henderson's tree house was filled with Katy Sloan pictures, CDs, fan magazines—even a Katy bobblehead!

Suddenly Nancy saw something tacked to a bulletin board. It was another picture of Katy Sloan, but this one was extra special. . . .

"You guys!" Nancy said, pointing to the bulletin board. "It's a picture of Katy Sloan— from our lemonade stand!"

Chapter

PAGE PUZZLER

Nancy, Bess, and George studied the picture.

"It's ours, all right," Bess said. She pointed to the picture. "There's the date of the concert I wrote on it!"

"So that's what Henderson stuffed in his pocket." Nancy sighed. "Not Hannah's recipe—*our* picture of Katy!"

"Henderson still could have taken our recipe," George insisted. "He needs thirty whole flavors of lemonade!"

"Henderson never tasted our lemonade," Nancy said. "And there were no strawberries in the garage anywhere!"

"Here's why!" Bess called out.

Nancy and George turned to see Bess holding a red rubber bracelet in her hand.

"It's an allergy bracelet!" Bess said. "It has a cartoony strawberry face on it and it says 'Allergic to Strawberries'!"

"Henderson is allergic to strawberries?" George wondered out loud.

"That's why there were no strawberries in the garage," Nancy said. "And why Henderson didn't drink our lemonade!"

"So Henderson is clean," George decided. "Now can we leave before those lemon-squirting squirts find us here?"

Leaving their Katy Sloan picture on the bulletin board, the Clue Crew climbed down from the tree house.

"Thirty flavors of lemonade," Bess said as they left the Murphy yard. "Do you think they'll have chocolate-chip lemonade, too?"

Nancy's eyes grew wide. The words "chocolate chip" made her remember something important.

"I have to go home right away," Nancy said. "I promised my dad I'd walk Chocolate Chip."

"What about our case?" Bess asked.

"There's no case left," George said with a frown. "Henderson was our last suspect."

Nancy frowned too. With no more suspects or clues, how would they find out who took

Hannah's secret recipe? And how long could she keep the truth from Hannah?

Nancy hoped Hannah wouldn't ask about the lemonade stand when she got home. But she had no such luck.

"No lemonade again today?" Hannah asked. "How come?"

"Um . . . we couldn't sell lemonade today, Hannah," Nancy said, pretending to itch and scratch. "There were too many mosquitoes outside!"

Hannah shrugged, then walked back to the kitchen.

Nancy felt horrible as she hooked Chip's leash onto her collar. Why couldn't she just tell Hannah that someone took her top-secret recipe?

"Daddy?" Nancy asked as he walked by. "When is it a good time to give up on a detective case?"

"Give up?" Mr. Drew said. He smiled and

shook his head. "Sometimes the real answer to a mystery is the one you least expect. So keep at it."

Nancy never did like to give up. And neither did the Clue Crew.

"Okay, Daddy," Nancy said, grabbing the Clue Book and pen. "Then I'd better take these on our walk!"

Once outside Nancy walked Chip up the path to the sidewalk. While her puppy sniffed at the flowers, Nancy opened the Clue Book. But as she flipped through the last few pages she froze.

Something was weird. Terribly weird!

"Omigosh, Chip!" Nancy gasped. "I know I wrote in my Clue Book, but now it's . . . it's . . . empty!"

Clue Crew—and
YOU!

Can you solve the mystery of the missing lemonade recipe? Write your answers in the Clue Book below. Or just turn the page to find out!

Nancy, Bess, and George came up with three suspects. Can you think of more? List your suspects.

1.
2.
3.

Write the way you think Hannah's top-secret recipe disappeared.

What clues helped you solve this mystery? Write them down below.

1.
2.
3.

Chapter

10

SURPRISE CUSTOMER

Nancy stared at each blank page. Everything had vanished like some magic trick!

"Our suspects and clues disappeared, Chip," Nancy said, tapping an empty page with the pen. "Just like the heart I drew on the kitchen calendar!"

Nancy stopped tapping to stare at the pen. It was the same pen she had used on the kitchen calendar. It was George's Presto Pen from her spy-girl kit!

That's when everything began to click. . . .

"I also used this pen to write Hannah's secret recipe!" Nancy said excitedly. "George may not know what the Presto Pen does, Chip. But I think I do!"

Nancy ran back into the house to phone her best friends. In a flash she and Bess were at George's door.

"I'll explain everything after I read the instructions for the Presto Pen," Nancy said. "Did you find them, George?"

George nodded and said, "The instructions were actually still inside the box."

But when the girls entered George's room, they froze. Sitting on the floor and scribbling all over the spy girl kit instructions was George's three-year-old brother, Scott!

"Scotty, no!" George said. "Give it back!"

Scotty put down his blue crayon. He pointed to the shiny charm bracelet circling Bess's wrist and said, "Give me that first. The *dragon* one!"

Bess whipped her hand back. "It's a unicorn!" she said. "And you can't have it, Scotty!"

Scott pouted and scrunched the instructions inside his fist. He was about to cry when—

"Give it to him, Bess, please!" Nancy said.

"Yeah, Bess!" George snapped. "You've got a million of those girly-girl things!"

Rolling her eyes, Bess snapped off the charm and handed it to Scotty. In turn,

Scotty handed George the instructions.

After unscrunching the instructions, George read about the Presto Pen out loud: "'The Presto Pen writes a supersecret message with ink that disappears within twenty-four hours. Now you see it. Now you don't!'"

"It's disappearing ink?" Bess exclaimed.

"Just as I thought!" Nancy said happily. "I used the Presto Pen to circle my calendar, write in the Clue Book, *and* write Hannah's secret recipe for pink-strawberry lemonade!"

"Wow, Nancy!" George said. "Are you saying—"

"Hannah's top-secret recipe was never stolen!" Nancy said excitedly. "It—poof—disappeared!"

"Poof!" Scotty laughed.

The Clue Crew traded big high fives. Hannah's top-secret recipe was out of sight but totally safe. They could ask Hannah to write it down again after they explained everything. And best of all . . .

"Our lemonade stand is back in business!" Nancy declared with a smile. "Katy Sloan tickets, here we come!"

Early the next day the Clue Crew sat behind their lemonade stand, happy to have solved another case. While Nancy stirred a pitcher of lemonade, a truck rolled by. It was the Mr. Drippy ice-cream truck!

"Guess what?" Henderson called from the truck. "My dad decided to keep his ice-cream truck after all. How awesome is that?"

"Awesome!" the girls called back.

They watched as the truck rolled away, playing the Mr. Drippy jingle. They were happy for Henderson, but not for themselves.

"We still haven't earned enough money for Katy Sloan tickets," Nancy said sadly. "And the concert is tomorrow."

"You guys," George said. "Maybe we should just forget about—"

"Katy Sloan!" Bess gasped.

Nancy and George followed Bess's gaze and gasped too. Stepping out of a sleek white car was the singer herself. It was Katy Sloan!

Nancy's heart pounded inside her chest as the star walked toward their lemonade stand. Katy Sloan smiled and said, "Hi."

"Y-y-you're Katy Sloan!" Nancy stammered.

"I'm in River Heights for my concert tomorrow," Katy said nicely. "I've been rehearsing all day, so I could use a cold cup of lemonade."

"We have lemonade!" George blurted.

"Pink-strawberry lemonade!" Nancy said.

"It's awesome!" Bess squeaked.

"Great!" Katy said. "One cup, please."

Nancy's hands shook as she poured Katy a cup of lemonade. The girls watched wide-eyed as their favorite singer drank. Did she like it?

"Oh, wow!" Katy said after drinking the last drop. "This is the best pink-strawberry lemonade I've ever tasted!"

"Would you like another cup?" Nancy asked.

"No, thank you," Katy said dropping a dollar into the jar. "But here's a little something extra."

The girls watched as Katy dropped three small red cards into the jar too. She gave a little wave and walked back to her car.

As the car drove off, Nancy pulled out the red cards. She looked at them and then let out a big shriek.

"Omigosh! Omigosh!" Nancy cried. "Three tickets to Katy's concert at the amusement park tomorrow!"

Nancy, Bess, and George couldn't stop

jumping and shrieking. They were going to the Katy Sloan concert!

"Nancy, George," Bess said as she stopped jumping. "We forgot to ask Katy Sloan for her autograph!"

"We can try tomorrow," George said.

"For sure!" Nancy said with a big smile. "But this time I'm bringing a *real* pen!"

Sparkle Spa

Making friends one Sparkly nail at a time!

EBOOK EDITIONS ALSO AVAILABLE

From Aladdin • KIDS.SimonandSchuster.com